Copyright © 2002 by Nord-Süd Verlag AG, Gossau Zürich, Switzerland
First published in Switzerland under the title *Maxi, der Schüchterne*.

English translation copyright © 2002 by North-South Books Inc., New York

All rights reserved. No part of this book may be reproduced or utilized in
any form or by any means, electronic or mechanical, including photocopying,
recording, or any information storage and retrieval system, without permission
in writing from the publisher.

First published in the United States, Great Britain, Canada,
Australia, and New Zealand in 2002 by North-South Books,
an imprint of Nord-Süd Verlag AG, Gossau Zürich, Switzerland.

Distributed in the United States by North-South Books Inc., New York.

Library of Congress Cataloging-in-Publication Data is available.
A CIP catalogue record for this book is available from The British Library.
ISBN 0-7358-1710-3 (trade edition) 10 9 8 7 6 5 4 3 2 1
ISBN 0-7358-1711-1 (library edition) 10 9 8 7 6 5 4 3 2 1
Printed in Germany

For more information about our books, and the authors and artists
who create them, visit our web site: www.northsouth.com

SHY GUY

By Gilles Tibo
Illustrated by Pef

Translated by
Sibylle Kazeroid

North-South Books
New York / London

My name is Greg,
but everybody
called me Red.
In the schoolyard,
at the park, in the street, people said,
"Hello, Red. How are you, Red?" I never
answered. I was shy. I had trouble with words.
They got stuck in my throat. When I tried to
talk, I choked up and blushed.

I had trouble with numbers, too.

If someone asked me, "How much is seven plus four minus two?" the numbers got all scrambled in my head. The sevens bumped into the fours, and the fours crashed into the twos. And of course I blushed bright red.

That's why people
called me Red,
and that's why
I hated
everything
red:
tomatoes,
radishes,
red apples,
red pencils,
red shirts,
red bicycles,
fires . . .

One day my parents asked me what I wanted for my birthday.

I blushed and said, "Umm. Maybe a very small goldfish . . . "

At the store, I couldn't believe what I did—I chose a red goldfish—even though I hated red!

He was the smallest goldfish they had, and the shyest one, too. He kept hiding at the bottom of the aquarium.
I felt sorry for him.
I named my goldfish Shy Guy.
We were shy together.

I set the fishbowl on my desk.
   For days we didn't talk. We just watched
one another.
   Finally, I spoke—one word . . . two words . . .
three words . . .

And Shy Guy replied—one bubble . . . two bubbles . . . three bubbles . . .
After that I told him jokes.
Guy made lots of bubbles when he laughed.

Then I showed Guy around my room. "This is my bed. Here is my teddy bear, my chair, my plane, my secret hiding place under the bed . . ."

Carefully, so I wouldn't spill any water on the floor, I showed him the rest of the house.

Guy was so excited that he spun around like a top.

I took him outside to show him around town.
I was a little bit nervous and embarrassed.
But Guy wanted to see everything. He opened his eyes wide.

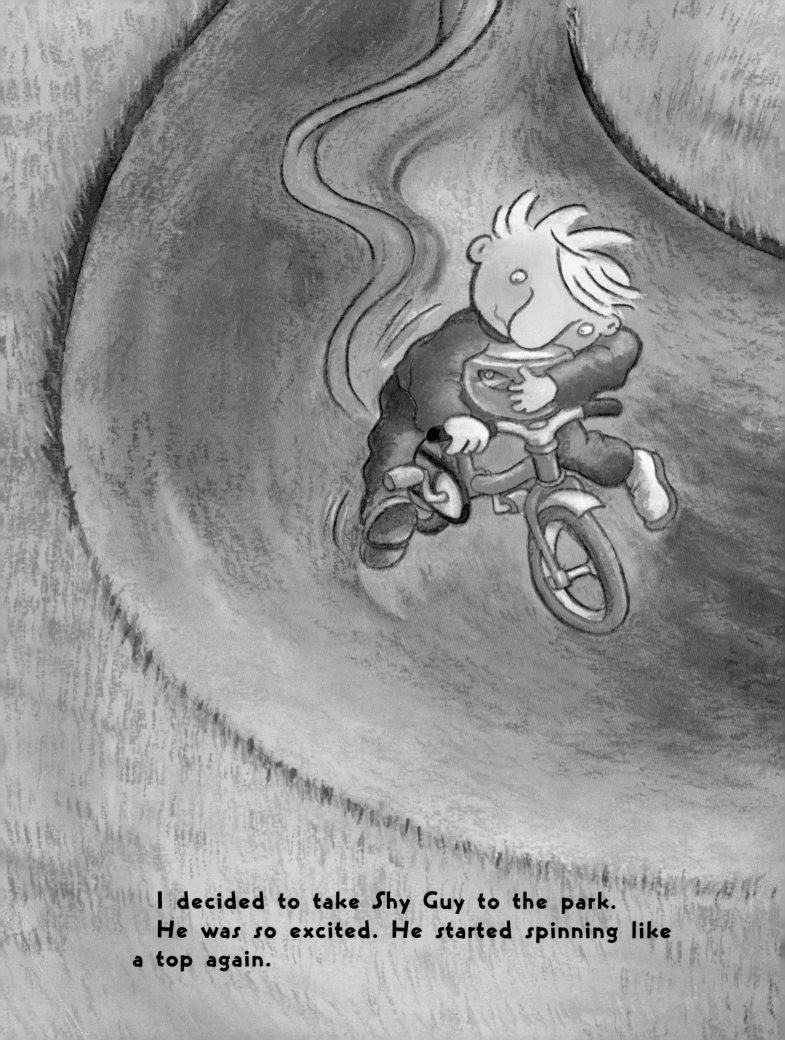

I decided to take Shy Guy to the park.
He was so excited. He started spinning like
a top again.

As soon as we got there, some kids rushed up to us.
"Is that a real goldfish, or is it plastic?"
"What's his name?"
"How old is he?"
"Does he drink a lot of water?"

I ran off to the swings so
I wouldn't have to answer.

Shy Guy loved the swings.
He did fantastic back flips.

Then Guy wanted to go on the slide.
I was at the top of the slide, trapped between those curious kids on the ladder behind me and those down at the bottom. But Guy wanted to slide, so I gave him a push! And suddenly the words came out in spite of myself: "He's a real live goldfish. . . . His name is Shy Guy. . . . He's three months old. . . .He doesn't drink much water. . . . quick, quick, catch him!"

Guy burst out laughing. He made lots and lots of bubbles.

The kids thought he was great.

The next day when I had to leave for school,
Guy looked sad and shy again. He just lay at the
bottom of his bowl and didn't make any bubbles.
I felt sorry for him, so I took him with me.

At school, everyone rushed up to us. They all wanted to see my fish.

"Well, look at this!" said my teacher. "How nice. Today, Greg, you can give a little speech and tell us all about your goldfish."

Oh no! I thought and started blushing.

In the classroom, I put Guy's bowl on my desk and tried to hide behind it so the teacher would forget about that speech.

It didn't work. Just before lunch, the teacher called me to the front of the classroom.

My heart beat very fast . . . my throat closed up . . . my head was spinning . . .

But suddenly, my throat opened up and all the words came unstuck. I talked and talked and talked about Shy Guy, right until the lunch bell rang—and I didn't blush a bit! It was the best day of my life!

I'm hardly *shy* at all anymore.
I talk to everyone, and everyone talks to me.
My friends come to play at my house, and sometimes they bring *their* pets.
Guy is the most extraordinary one—he can make bubbles!